Disney

Anna & Elsa

A Warm Welcome

To sisters everywhere.
May the magic of Anna and Elsa
always be yours!
—E.D.

randomhousekids.com

ISBN 978-0-7364-3289-4 (hardcover) — ISBN 978-0-7364-8247-9 (lib. bdg.)

Printed in the United States of America
10 9 8 7 6 5 4 3 2 1

Disney

Anna & Elsa

A Warm Welcome

By Erica David
Illustrated by Bill Robinson,
Manuela Razzi, Francesco Legramandi,
and Gabriella Matta

Random House New York

Chapter 1

It was a crisp winter day in Arendelle, and Queen Elsa was returning to her castle. She had just finished a long day of bringing supplies and gifts to her villagers. She had delivered a box of new saws and picks to the ice harvesters. She'd brought blankets and hot soup to the stable boys. She had even given books to the schoolchildren.

Elsa smiled. She loved helping people. She felt more like a queen every day.

Suddenly, a snowball sailed right over her head.

"Hello?" Elsa called out. She hopped down from her horse and looked around, but no one was there. Then she heard a rustling in the bushes nearby. It was Olaf, the walking, talking snowman.

"Sorry, Elsa!" Olaf said with a giggle. "I was just having a snowball fight with Sven."

"That's okay, Olaf," Elsa said, laughing and shaking snow from her hair. She didn't bother to ask him how a reindeer could throw a snowball.

Sven poked his head out from behind

a tree and snorted happily. Elsa was glad she had remembered to bring carrots with her. Carrots were Sven's favorite food. She pulled one from her bag and let the reindeer take a bite. Sven nuzzled her in appreciation.

"Oh, isn't Arendelle wonderful, Elsa?" Olaf asked, opening his stick arms wide with glee. "I just love snowball fights, and sledding, and playing with Sven."

Elsa looked around. Snow-covered branches sparkled in the sunlight. Icicles twinkled. Arendelle really was beautiful this time of year.

"Although it is awfully *white*," Olaf continued, "and cold. *Brrr.* That's why I *really* love summer. Oh, wouldn't it be fun

to travel to Summer Land? We could meet the Summer Queen and see her tropical magic!"

Elsa chuckled at Olaf's joke. "Tropical magic," she said, nodding. "That *would* be nice, wouldn't it?"

"No, really," Olaf said. "I was visiting with the ice harvesters, and they were all talking about the kingdom of Eldora, where it's always summer!"

Elsa was puzzled. She was familiar with most of the neighboring kingdoms, but she had never heard of the kingdom of Eldora. "Really?" she asked.

"Uh-huh!" Olaf said merrily. "The Queen of Eldora can control fire and heat! Just like your ice and snow magic!"

Elsa was intrigued. She'd never met anyone with magical powers. She enjoyed the idea that maybe there was someone else like her in the world.

"Can you imagine?" Olaf said, talking to himself. "Oh, I just love summer, and

the sun, and everything warm, and—"

"Olaf?" Elsa interrupted. "Are you sure it's *always* summer in Eldora?"

Olaf nodded. "Isn't it great?"

Elsa agreed and climbed back on her horse. She had royal duties to attend to at the castle. But as she traveled across the snowbanks, she became completely lost in her thoughts. Could there really be a Summer Land? Did the queen of Summer Land really have magical powers? Elsa was so distracted that she almost ran right into Fritz, the innkeeper. He was busy loading firewood onto a large sled.

"Sorry, Fritz!" Elsa said, peering at him from her saddle. "I almost didn't see you down there."

"That's all right, Your Majesty," Fritz said with a bow. "How are you on this fine afternoon?"

"Fritz?" Elsa said, sliding down from her horse. "Have you ever heard of the kingdom of Eldora?"

"Why, yes, Your Majesty," Fritz said. "Just last week, a foreign merchant came to stay at the inn. He had recently returned from Eldora. He said it was one of the warmest places on earth."

Elsa felt a twinge of excitement. It sounded as though Olaf had been right. "So," she said to Fritz carefully, "it was still summer in Eldora, then? When this merchant went for a visit?"

"Your Majesty," Fritz said kindly, "I

think it's fair to say that in Eldora, it's *always* summer."

Elsa thought back to the time she had accidentally set off an eternal winter in Arendelle. It wasn't that she'd wanted to freeze the summer or run away to the North Mountain. She definitely hadn't liked shutting out her younger sister, Anna. It was just that avoiding everyone had seemed like the only way to be herself *and* keep her friends safe. She hadn't yet learned how to control her powers.

That was when it hit her. *This Summer Queen might not know how to control her powers, either.* How else could you explain an eternal summer?

Elsa wasn't sure what she was going to

do, but she knew she needed some help.

"I'll see you later, Fritz!" Elsa said. With that, she jumped back on her horse and galloped away at full speed, all the way to the castle.

Elsa found Anna in her room, admiring a portrait of a woman wearing shining armor.

"Oh, Elsa!" Anna said. Her face lit up when she saw her sister. "I'm so glad you're here. I just had this painting moved to my room. Isn't it great?"

"Anna!" Elsa said abruptly. "You'll never believe what Olaf told me!" She quickly and carefully told her sister what she'd heard about the Summer Queen and her tropical magic.

"I can't believe it!" Anna exclaimed when Elsa had finished. "It's just like the time you set off an eternal winter in Arendelle."

"Exactly," Elsa said, nodding. "I think we should send a royal emissary to bring back information. What do you think?"

"Hmm." Anna looked a little disappointed. "I thought you were going to say that *we* should go."

Elsa was surprised. She hadn't considered traveling to Eldora herself. After all, she had villagers to take care of and a kingdom to run. She couldn't just leave everyone.

Anna went to Elsa's side and gently took her hand. "If this Summer Queen really doesn't know how to control her powers, then surely *you* are the best person to help her."

Anna had a good point. "Maybe," Elsa said cautiously. "But I have no idea where Eldora is. How would we even get there?"

Anna paced back and forth across her room, thinking. "I've got it!" she said suddenly. "Come on!"

Anna grabbed Elsa by the hand and pulled her down the hall to the library. She searched through her father's collection of books until she found what she was looking for—an atlas.

Inside the atlas were maps of all the neighboring kingdoms. She quickly flipped through the pages.

"Here it is!" she cried.

Elsa looked at the dingy, fraying map. First she found Arendelle. Then she traced her finger across the sea until she found Eldora.

It would be a very long journey.

Sometimes being a queen involved difficult decisions. Elsa plopped down in her father's old armchair and sighed.

"Oh, Elsa," Anna said. "We *have* to help the Summer Queen. Just imagine how different things would be if you never had anyone around to help you."

Elsa thought about it. She knew how lucky she was to have a sister, someone who could help her make important decisions. She wondered if the Summer Queen had a sister, too. Or did she have to run the kingdom of Eldora all by herself?

"Let me discuss this with Kai," Elsa said finally. "I need to be certain that the ministers can handle things while we're gone."

She summoned Kai, the royal butler, and explained her plans.

"The ministers and I would be happy to watch over the villagers in your absence," Kai said.

Anna's eyes widened with anticipation. "So, what do you say, Elsa?" she asked.

"I do like helping people," Elsa said quietly.

"Of course you do! That's why you're such a wonderful queen," Anna said.

"Besides, we can do anything if we do it together."

Elsa smiled. She knew Anna was right.

"Kai, ready the ship!" Elsa said. "We're going to save Eldora and help the Summer Queen!"

Kai bowed. "Right away, Your Majesty."

Anna squealed with delight.

For the next several days, all of Arendelle was busy helping Anna and Elsa prepare for their trip. Maids helped the sisters pack some clothes. Villagers presented Anna and Elsa with gifts of bread and meat and cakes. Then, just as the sisters were preparing to leave for the docks, Olaf burst into Elsa's room.

"Can I come, too?" he asked. "I just love summer!"

Anna giggled. Elsa gently patted Olaf's head. "Of course, Olaf," she said. "You can come, too."

Chapter 2

The Arendelle docks were crowded with villagers. To Elsa, it seemed as though everyone in town had come to wish her and her sister a safe journey. Women waved handkerchiefs in the air. Men hoisted children onto their shoulders. A crew of sailors carried trunk after trunk up the gangplank, loading the ship with everything Elsa and Anna would need for their trip.

Elsa and Anna walked arm in arm through the crush of people. Elsa couldn't help smiling. She was excited to travel to Eldora. She hoped she and the Summer Queen would become friends.

When the sisters arrived at the ship, Elsa turned to face the townspeople. She had prepared a short speech. She wanted to thank them for their kindness and help. She also wanted to assure them that she would not be gone for long. But just as she was about to speak, she felt a sharp tug on the sleeve of her dress.

It was Anna. She looked worried.

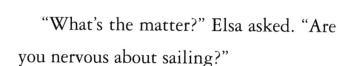

"What's the matter?" Elsa asked. "Are you nervous about sailing?"

Anna shook her head. "No. I just realized how much I'm going to miss Kristoff and Sven."

Elsa felt a pang of sadness. She had been so busy making preparations for the trip that she hadn't stopped to consider how much she would miss her friends, too. She looked up at the big wooden ship. *There is plenty of room for two more travelers,* she thought.

Elsa smiled and put her arm around Anna's shoulders. "Quick, go ask Kristoff and Sven if they would like to see Eldora, too."

"Really?" Anna said.

Elsa nodded and gave Anna a wink.

"Yes!" Anna said, clasping her hands together in gratitude. "I'll be right back!" She dashed off into the crowd to share the good news.

Elsa, Anna, and Olaf stood on the ship's deck, waving goodbye to the villagers of Arendelle below. Meanwhile, Kristoff and Sven had decided to assist the crew. There was plenty of work to be done. Kristoff helped one group of sailors raise the anchor. Sven hoisted the mainsail with another group. Elsa watched in wonder as a giant white sail inched up the mast and began to billow in the breeze.

"Heave-ho! Away we go!" cried the ship's captain.

The ship slowly began to drift out to sea. The people waiting on the docks waved wildly and called out good wishes.

As they sailed farther and farther away from Arendelle, Elsa began to notice changes in scenery. In the fjord, she was used to seeing snowcapped mountains and glaciers floating in the icy blue water. Now she couldn't see any snow at all. And the normally blue water was almost green. It was turquoise!

Elsa took a deep breath of salty sea air. High above her, a seagull flew in a loop-the-loop.

"Isn't it beautiful, Anna?" she asked.

She had never been this far from home. She was beginning to see how big the world really was, and she was looking forward to exploring.

"It *is* beautiful!" Anna said. "In fact, I'm going to get an even better view!"

Elsa watched as Anna's gaze moved up the mainsail. At the very top was a wooden platform, tied to the mast with heavy rope. By standing on the platform, a sailor could see into the distance and look out to faraway lands.

"You're going to climb that?" Elsa asked, a hint of concern creeping into her voice.

Anna's face broke into a mischievous grin. "Don't worry, Elsa. I'll be careful."

Elsa watched as Anna marched over to the mast. Anna grabbed the rope ladder with both hands. Then she picked up one foot and carefully placed it on the lowest rung.

"Excuse me, Your Highness," Kristoff said, suddenly appearing at Anna's side. "Don't you think that *I* should be the one to climb all the way up there?" He jokingly flexed his muscles. Sven, standing next to Olaf near the back of the ship, gave a cheerful snort.

"Kristoff, I'm perfectly capable of climbing a rope ladder," Anna said, chuckling. She pulled herself up to the next rung on the ladder. Then she picked up her left foot and climbed higher. She was reaching for the next rung when she started to slip.

"Oh, no!" Elsa cried. She held her breath.

Kristoff stretched out his arms, ready to catch Anna if she fell. But to everyone's surprise, Anna started to laugh.

"Just kidding," she said.

Everyone breathed a sigh of relief.

Anna climbed to the top of the mast and carefully stepped onto the platform.

"Elsa, Kristoff—this view is amazing!" she called. "I can see for miles in every direction!" Anna turned in a slow circle, taking in the impressive view, then stopped and pointed straight out to sea.

"Look!" she cried. "Dolphins!"

Elsa and Kristoff turned and saw a pod of dolphins swimming faster and faster toward the ship.

"I've always wanted to see a dolphin!" Olaf said. He sprinted across the deck. His little cloud flurry bobbed above his head. "Hello, dolphins! My name is Olaf, and I like warm—"

Suddenly, Olaf slipped on a rope and went flying into the air!

It seemed to Elsa that Olaf was falling in slow motion. She knew if she didn't do something, he would fall right off the side of the ship and into the sea. She quickly opened her arms and summoned her magic. A slide made entirely of ice appeared in the air below Olaf. He fell onto the slide and slid down to land safely on the deck.

"*Whee!* That was fun!" Olaf exclaimed.

Elsa breathed another sigh of relief.

"That was close," Kristoff muttered.

Elsa nodded. After all the excitement, she was feeling a little tired. While she looked for a place to sit down, she saw the ship's captain approaching. He held his hat in his hands.

"Excuse me, Your Majesty," he said. "If you and your friends would like to go belowdecks, dinner is served."

"Great!" Kristoff said. "I'm starved!"

Sven snorted in agreement.

"Be right down!" Anna shouted from the lookout.

Elsa felt her stomach rumble. She was hungry, too. She started toward the eating and sleeping quarters, when a thought occurred to her. She turned back to the captain.

"What about the crew?" Elsa asked.

"We'll wait until you're finished. Then we'll eat," the captain said with a bow.

"Nonsense!" Elsa said. "We'll all eat together, as friends."

The captain broke into a wide smile. "Thank you, Your Majesty."

Belowdecks, Elsa watched happily as the Arendelle sailors shared their meal of soup, bread, and hot glögg. Some of them sang songs. Others shared stories of their travels.

Elsa smiled. Her journey was just beginning, but she couldn't wait to find out what tomorrow would bring.

Chapter 3

"Ahoy! Land ho!"

Elsa opened her eyes and sat up in her bunk with a start. *What was that sound?* She listened as hard as she could. All she could hear was Anna snoring.

"Land ho!"

There it was again. Elsa gasped. She suddenly realized it was one of the sailors alerting the crew. Someone had spotted Eldora in the distance!

"Anna! Wake up!" Elsa said, flying out of her bed.

Anna rubbed her eyes with her fists and yawned. "What is it?" she asked sleepily.

"We're almost there!" Elsa cried. "We've reached Summer Land!"

Anna jumped right out of bed. "Oh, finally!"

The last few days aboard the ship had been filled with adventure. Elsa had learned how to hoist the sails and batten down the hatches. But despite the fun she was having, she was eager to reach Eldora. She missed dry land. She also couldn't wait to meet the Summer Queen. Elsa and Anna quickly changed out of their nightclothes. They joined everyone else on deck.

Elsa said good morning to Kristoff, Sven, and the captain. Then she put her hand to her forehead to block the sun. In the distance, she could see a thin stretch of brown land. She felt a drop of sweat slide down her cheek and drip onto her neck.

"This heat!" Elsa said, turning to Anna. "I've never felt anything like it!"

Anna was squinting. She waved her hand in front of her face like a fan. "I know," she said. "It's so hot! And the sun is so bright! It's so . . . it's so . . ."

"Summery?" Olaf said with a giggle.

The sisters looked over at Olaf. He had

a huge smile on his face, perfectly cool beneath his very own snow flurry.

"Yes, Olaf," Elsa said, laughing. "It's very summery."

Just then, a huge gust of wind billowed the sails. The ship rolled in the waves. The crew worked feverishly to keep it steady. Elsa was surprised to notice that the wind was not cool and refreshing, like it was in Arendelle. This wind was hot. She didn't feel refreshed at all. In fact, she felt even warmer when it blew.

"Could this be the work of the Summer Queen?" Anna whispered to Elsa.

"I don't know," Elsa said, looking around at the sailors. Everyone was working very hard. They were sweating a lot, too. "But I've got to do something to keep people cool in this heat."

Elsa tapped her foot on the ship's deck. In an instant, the deck was covered with a thin layer of snow. The air immediately felt cooler. Elsa smiled. But her smile soon turned into a frown. Each time the ship rocked in the waves, sailors would slip and

slide from one end of the boat to the other. They struggled to keep their balance. One of them even tripped on a snowdrift and fell on his rump!

Kristoff, standing next to Elsa, crossed his arms and raised an eyebrow. "I don't think that's going to work," he said under his breath.

"You're right," Elsa agreed. She tapped her foot again. In a matter of moments, all of the snow disappeared.

Elsa looked around. A young sailor named Bjarne was carrying a large carafe of hot glögg. She motioned for him to approach her. In Arendelle, hot glögg kept the sailors toasty and warm in the snowy weather. But in sunny Eldora, it was just too hot to drink.

Elsa raised her hands and the carafe magically filled with ice cubes. She smiled again. "That should work," she said confidently. But to her surprise, the ice cubes immediately began to melt.

"What's wrong with your magic, Elsa?" Anna asked, concerned.

"Nothing's wrong," Elsa said. "It's just that keeping everyone cool is harder than I thought it would be."

The sisters exchanged a worried look. Could it be that the Summer Queen's magic was even more powerful than Elsa's?

Elsa scratched her head and tried to think it through. Then she heard Olaf talking to Sven. Olaf was going on and on about how much he loved summer. Elsa smiled. She loved that Olaf was always cheerful. He was also kind. And he loved warm hugs.

That was when Elsa got an idea. "Everyone!" she cried. "Hug Olaf!"

Most of the sailors looked at Elsa like she was crazy. But she rushed over to Olaf, dropped down on one knee, and gave him a big, sweet hug. She breathed yet another sigh of relief as her body cooled.

"Elsa! You're a genius!" Anna exclaimed. She ran over to give Olaf a hug, too.

Kristoff chuckled. "Nice work, Elsa," he said. He walked over and stretched out his arms in Olaf's direction. "Come here, buddy."

"Aww, you guys," Olaf said, delighted by all the attention. "I like you, too!"

Olaf gave Kristoff a nuzzle. Then he stretched out his stick arms and turned to face the rest of the crew. "Well," he said, excited. "Who's next?"

One by one, the sailors took turns hugging the snowman. With a body made entirely of snow and protected by his very own cloud flurry, Olaf was the only cold thing on the ship.

Chapter 4

"Your Majesty," the captain said to Elsa, "we'll have to drop anchor here."

Elsa nodded. They had finally reached Eldora's harbor. The water was dotted with small, brightly colored fishing boats. Teams of Eldoran fishermen hauled nets filled with wriggling fish on board. Behind the boats, Elsa could see the coast.

"How will we get to shore?" she asked the captain.

He pointed to a small wooden rowboat on the ship's deck. "We'll lower the rowboat into the water. One of my sailors will row you and your friends to shore."

"Thank you," Elsa said kindly.

The sailors worked together, slowly lowering the small boat into the water. Then they hung a rope ladder off the side of the ship. One by one, Anna, Elsa, Olaf, and Kristoff climbed down the ladder and stepped into the rowboat. Elsa looked back up at the mighty ship. Sven was still standing on the deck.

"It's okay, Sven!" Kristoff hollered. "Just jump. I'll catch you."

Sven raised one of his bushy eyebrows. Then he backed up a few paces. With a running start, Sven leapt off the ship. He landed safely in the rowboat, but he created a giant splash! Kristoff, Anna, and Elsa got soaked.

"Well, I finally feel refreshed," Anna said, laughing and wringing water from her hair.

As one of the sailors began to row, Elsa looked out across the harbor. She took note of how different things were in Eldora. There were no snowcapped mountains or grassy fields. The land looked very flat. Also, the fishermen were dressed in unusual clothing. Instead of fur-trimmed vests and wool pants like Kristoff's, they wore long, flowing shirts. Some of them wore colorful scarves wrapped around their heads.

Elsa touched her white-blond braid. She looked at Anna's red hair.

"No one in Eldora looks like us," Elsa whispered to her sister. It seemed as though everyone in Eldora had dark brown or black hair.

Anna nodded. "I know. No one is wearing a magical dress, either."

Elsa looked down at her sparkly blue dress. She looked back at her sister, and the girls burst into a fit of giggles.

Meanwhile, Olaf was overcome with excitement. "Oh, Summer Land is just like I imagined!" he said with glee. "It's so warm and sunny!" He waved merrily to the fishermen.

The fishermen of Eldora stared back, wide-eyed in disbelief.

"You know, Elsa," Anna said, leaning closer to her sister, "I don't think the fishermen of Eldora have ever seen a snowman before." She lowered her voice. "Especially not one who can walk and talk!"

"Anna," Elsa said, smiling, "I think you're right."

*

Elsa stepped out of the rowboat and onto dry land. Right away, she sensed trouble.

"This place looks just like Arendelle did when you set off that eternal winter,

Elsa," Anna said. "But instead of a blanket of snow, Eldora is covered in sand!"

Anna was right. No grass, no trees, no bushes, and no shrubs. With each step Elsa took, her foot sank into the sand. It *was* an awful lot like walking on snow, only warmer.

"This is more serious than I thought," she said. "I'm glad we came."

"Wait for me!" Olaf called behind them.

Elsa turned to see Olaf surrounded by a group of Eldoran fishermen. Each of them took turns giving him a hug. Then they tossed him joyfully in the air. Olaf had already made some new friends. Elsa could hear him giggling all the way down the beach.

Elsa waited for Olaf to catch up. "Isn't it wonderful?" he said after rejoining the group from Arendelle. "It's so hot!"

"Probably a little *too* hot," Kristoff said. He took off his vest and draped it over his shoulder.

"I love summer!" Olaf said cheerfully.

Elsa looked at Anna. She let out a small sigh. "I think Olaf loves summer so much, he can't see the trouble with an *eternal* summer," she whispered. "In fact, I'm not sure Olaf sees trouble in much of anything." She patted him gently on the head.

Farther up the beach, Elsa and her friends came across a young fishmonger. He was loading fish into a wheeled cart.

"Hello," the fishmonger said with a smile. "I'm Kamal. Welcome to Eldora!"

"Nice to meet you, Kamal," Kristoff said.

"Yeah, nice to meet you, Kamal," Olaf echoed. He stretched out his stick arms. "Would you like a hug, too?"

Kamal let out a surprised yelp. Obviously, he had never seen a snowman before, either.

Kristoff smiled. "Don't worry about Olaf," he said. "He's harmless." Kristoff reached over to shake Kamal's hand. But a puzzled look suddenly spread across his face.

"Where's your ice?" Kristoff asked. He pointed to the fish in Kamal's cart, which was baking in the hot Eldora sun.

Elsa knew that in Arendelle, fish was always packed in ice. That way it stayed fresh for a long time. But when she peered into Kamal's cart, she didn't see any ice anywhere.

"Ice?" Kamal said. "I *wish*. We don't have ice in Eldora. We keep our fish fresh with water from the sea." With that, Kamal poured a bucket of salty seawater right on top of the fish.

"No ice in Eldora?" Kristoff said. He looked stunned.

Sven snorted in agreement. What a strange land Eldora was turning out to be.

"Kamal, I'm Queen Elsa of Arendelle," Elsa said.

Kamal's eyes grew wide and he dropped into a low bow. "Please forgive me, Your Majesty," he said. "I didn't know I was speaking with royalty."

Elsa smiled kindly. Sometimes she forgot that most people weren't used to meeting a queen. She gently took Kamal by the arm and raised him from his bow.

"My friends and I are here to meet the Summer Queen," she said. "We'd like to help rid Eldora of its eternal summer!"

Kamal looked at Elsa strangely. "Well, it certainly *feels* eternal," he said, wiping sweat from his brow. "But the castle is several days' journey from here. And the gates to the royal city aren't even open."

Elsa was surprised. She looked at Anna, not sure what to do next.

"It's just like back when our parents decided to shut the gates of Arendelle!" Anna whispered.

Elsa closed her eyes and thought back to a time long before, when Arendelle's gates were closed. She was never allowed outside the palace. She hardly ever saw her sister. It had been safer for her to avoid everyone entirely. She had also been terribly lonely. Elsa felt sorry for the Summer Queen. She was probably lonely, too.

"Kamal?" Elsa asked, opening her eyes. "Can you tell us how to get to the castle?"

"Certainly, Your Majesty," Kamal said. "First, you'll want to stop at the marketplace. You can purchase supplies for your travels there." He pointed to a bustling open-air market not far from the beach.

Sven whinnied and nuzzled his head against Kristoff's arm.

"Yes, I'm sure they have carrots at the market," Kristoff whispered to the hungry reindeer.

"All right," Elsa said to Kamal. "Then what?"

"Then you'll cross the Eldora desert.

It's a long journey." At this point, Kamal's eyes came to rest on Olaf. "Especially if you're, uh, traveling on foot."

"I love long journeys!" Olaf said innocently.

Meanwhile, Elsa shot Anna a worried look.

"Finally, you'll reach the hills of Eldora," Kamal continued. "That's where you'll find the castle."

"Thank you, Kamal," Elsa said. "You've been very helpful."

"Good luck with your fish!" Kristoff said.

Elsa and her friends waved goodbye to Kamal and walked on.

Chapter 5

To Elsa's delight, Eldora's marketplace was an explosion of colors and aromas. Stall after stall was filled with fruits, vegetables, fish, and meats. Others contained coffee and tea. Still more were piled high with exotic spices, such as bright orange saffron and deep red paprika. The rich scents wafted through the air, tickling Elsa's nose.

As she strolled through the market,
Elsa noticed the merchants smiling
brightly. "The people of Eldora are
certainly friendly," she said.

Anna nodded. "Well, I would be
friendly, too! Look at these amazing
carpets! And these fabrics and shoes!"

Anna skipped through the market.
There were handwoven rugs in every color
of the rainbow. There were leather goods—
belts and bags and purses. It seemed
the Eldora market contained everything
anyone could imagine. As she turned a
corner, Anna almost skipped right into
Kristoff. He was admiring a large wooden
wagon.

"Look at this craftsmanship," Kristoff

said, shaking his head in wonder. He carefully traced his finger along the beautifully carved wood. "This is almost as nice as my sled back home."

"It's lovely," Anna agreed. "But don't you think it's a little big for a souvenir?"

"No, silly," Kristoff chuckled. "Kamal said it would be a long journey on foot, remember? This way, Sven can pull us across the desert."

"That's a great idea, Kristoff!" Elsa chimed in. She turned to a nearby merchant. She wanted to buy the wagon for their journey. But just as she was going to say hello, the merchant's eyes widened in terror. He closed his shutters right in Elsa's face.

Elsa was confused. Everyone in Eldora had been so warm and welcoming. She was surprised to see someone act rudely.

"Elsa! Look!" Anna cried.

Elsa turned and saw a huge dark cloud in the distance.

"Is it a thunderstorm?" Anna asked.

Elsa shook her head. "It can't be." Elsa pointed at the cloud. Instead of being up in the sky, the cloud was hovering right above the ground.

Elsa looked down at her feet. Sand had started to blow around in the breeze. That was when she realized what the cloud meant—a sandstorm! Elsa wrapped her cloak around her face to shield her eyes.

"Oh, no!" Anna cried. "The Summer

Queen! She must be upset about something!"

"Her powers are obviously very strong," Elsa agreed.

"What should we do?" Anna asked.

Elsa looked around. She knew it was too late to buy the wagon—the merchants had closed their stalls and packed up their wares in a hurry. She also knew that she and her friends would need shelter when the sandstorm hit, but she didn't see any place to hide.

"We could try to outrun the storm," Kristoff suggested.

"Do you think that's possible?" Anna asked.

Kristoff shrugged. "Honestly, I'm not sure. But I think it might be worth a try. What do you all think?"

Anna nodded. Sven gave an encouraging snort. Olaf smiled. "Sounds exciting!" he said.

"I guess it's settled, then," Elsa said. "We'll have to continue on foot."

*

Elsa and her friends traveled as quickly as they could manage, trying to get ahead of the storm. But the longer they walked, the more concerned Elsa became. Every few moments, she looked over her shoulder. Even though it was the middle of the

afternoon, the sky was growing darker by the second. The storm cloud was gaining on them.

"I don't think we're going fast enough," Anna said. She pulled her cloak tighter around her head and face. "Maybe we should pick up the pace?"

"Maybe we should turn around!" Kristoff shouted. He had to raise his voice to be heard above the howling wind.

Elsa glanced over her shoulder again. She couldn't see the market anymore. In fact, she could barely see anything. She was just about to tell Kristoff when she stubbed her toe on something. *Hard.* "Ow!" she cried out. "What in the world?"

Elsa knelt and felt around in the

growing darkness. To her surprise, it was a wooden boat, upside down and abandoned in the sand.

"What's a boat doing in the middle of the desert?" Anna hollered.

"I don't know!" Elsa yelled back. It was getting harder and harder to see or hear.

All of a sudden, she felt her feet start to

rise off the ground. She was getting swept away by the wind!

"Anna!" Elsa cried. "Help!" She reached out to grab hold of her sister.

"I'm trying!" Anna hollered. She stretched out an arm, leapt into the air, and snatched Elsa's hand. "Gotcha!"

"Come on!" Kristoff yelled. "Follow me!"

Kristoff knelt in the sand and crawled beneath the boat. Elsa, Anna, and Sven followed. The upside-down boat was just like a little house. It was the perfect place to seek shelter from the storm.

"Wow! That was close," Anna said, shaking sand from her hair and dress.

Elsa nodded. "Another good idea,

Kristoff." She began to relax. Her sister, Sven, and Kristoff were all safe. Then Elsa turned in a panic.

"Oh, no!" she said. "Where's Olaf?"

Chapter 6

Elsa waited anxiously for the sandstorm to subside. It was too dangerous to look for Olaf while the storm was raging. When she could no longer hear the howling of the wind, Elsa crawled from the boat and into the light.

"Wow!" Elsa said. The sun was so bright, it was practically blinding. She blinked a few times. Then she looked around and let out a gasp. There was sand everywhere—as far as she could see in every direction!

Anna, Kristoff, and Sven crawled out and stood next to Elsa. Anna squinted. Kristoff raised a hand to his forehead to shield his eyes from the sun.

"And I thought there was a lot of sand on the beach!" Anna said.

"No kidding," said Kristoff. "This must be the desert Kamal told us about."

Kristoff walked over to Sven and fished a carrot from his pocket. Sven snorted and took a hungry bite.

"We must have wandered pretty far in the storm," Anna said. "I can't even see the market anymore."

"I know," Elsa said. "I can't see much of anything . . . except sand."

Elsa furrowed her brow. She was worried about Olaf. How would they ever find him in the middle of a desert?

Anna reached out and grabbed her sister's hand. "Don't worry, Elsa," she said. "We'll find him. Remember, Olaf loves summer."

Anna was right. Wherever he was, Olaf was probably loving the hot sand.

Elsa and her friends began racing up and down the sand dunes. They shouted Olaf's name and scanned the horizon.

"Look!" Kristoff shouted. "What is that?"

In the haze, Elsa could barely make

out a small, round object on top of one of the dunes. It was brown, the same color as the sand. In the distance, it looked like a statue.

"That's odd," Elsa said. "What could it be?"

"I don't know," Kristoff said. "Let's check it out!"

Elsa and her friends sprinted toward the object. As she got closer, Elsa began to realize that the statue looked a lot like Olaf. It had the same round body. It had the same pointy nose. She held her breath in anticipation.

"Olaf?" she said timidly. She tiptoed toward the figure until she was standing right next to it.

Suddenly, the statue started to move! Sand flew into the air and landed everywhere. Underneath the sand was something round and white. Olaf!

"Hi, guys!" Olaf said happily. He shook the rest of the sand from his body. His personal flurry popped up and hovered above his head. "Wow! Look at all this sand! I just love summer, don't you?"

Elsa, Anna, and Kristoff broke into hearty laughter. Olaf was all right.

The group trudged back across the dunes.

"I wonder why this is just sitting here," Kristoff said. He kicked the boat gently

with the tip of his shoe. "That's no way to take care of a boat."

"I know," Anna said. "It's so strange. Why would anyone leave a boat in the middle of the desert?"

"Do you think it has something to do with the Summer Queen?" Elsa asked.

Anna and Kristoff shrugged.

"Oh, look!" Olaf interrupted. "A lake!"

Elsa, Anna, and Kristoff peered into the distance. There, many miles away, was what appeared to be a sparkling blue lake. It glimmered in the haze.

"I guess that explains the boat," Kristoff said with a chuckle.

Elsa looked longingly at the lake. It

would be the perfect place to stop and rest. If only they still had that wagon.

Suddenly, Elsa had an idea.

"What if we flip this boat over," she said. "Then we can hook it up to Sven!"

"Just like a sled!" Kristoff said excitedly. "We can sit inside while Sven pulls us across the desert!"

"Great idea, Elsa!" Anna said.

Kristoff took two ropes from his rucksack. He tied one end of each rope to the boat. Then he tied the other ends to Sven's bridle. Before long, they were ready to continue on their journey.

"All aboard, ladies," Kristoff said merrily. He leaned over in a low bow.

"And gentleman," he added to Olaf. Olaf giggled.

Once everyone was safely inside the boat, Kristoff grabbed the reins. "Okay, Sven!" he called. "Let's go!"

Sven snorted and they were off, sledding across miles and miles of sand.

Before long, Elsa began to feel very tired. Running across the dunes had been exhausting. She stretched out on the bottom of the boat. She closed her eyes and let out a big yawn. Just as she began to drift off to sleep, she felt the boat slide to stop.

"Why are we stopping?" Elsa asked.

Kristoff looked around, confused.

"I don't understand," he said, scratching his head. "Where did the lake go?"

Elsa sat up and looked around. She was astonished. The lake had disappeared. There was only a dry, empty basin.

Chapter 7

"Maybe it was a mirage," Elsa said, disappointed.

"A mirage?" Anna asked. She plopped down on the shore of the dried-up lake.

"A mirage is a little like a magic trick," Elsa explained. "It's when you see things that aren't really there."

"Like a lake?" Kristoff said.

Elsa nodded. "Exactly."

"Some magic," Anna muttered. She lay back in the sand and covered her eyes with her hand.

"What's wrong, Anna?" Elsa asked.

Anna sat up and sighed. "This trip isn't turning out to be as much fun as I thought it would be," she said. She looked at Sven, who was panting in the heat. "It isn't safe. I think we should consider going home."

"But we're in Summer Land!" Olaf said. "Who could ever want to leave all this?" He waved his stick arms around.

Anna gave him a weak smile.

Elsa sat on the sand next to her sister.

It wasn't like Anna to give up. "I know you're frustrated," she said, "but the Summer Queen needs our help. If you hadn't traveled to the North Mountain to help me, Arendelle might still be trapped in an eternal winter! We can't let that happen to the people of Eldora."

A smile began to spread across Anna's face.

"You're the bravest person I know," Elsa continued. "We can do this together."

Anna sat up and threw her arms around her sister's neck. "Oh, Elsa, you're right," she said. "I'm sorry."

"More hugs!" Olaf said. He waddled over and placed his stick arms around the sisters. "Come on, Sven."

Sven let out a quiet whinny and joined the group hug, too.

"Uh, guys?" Kristoff interrupted.

"Just a minute, Kristoff," Anna said. "We're kind of having a moment here." She continued hugging her sister.

"Guys!" Kristoff said a little more urgently. "I think we need to go. *Now.*"

"What is it, Kri—"

Elsa turned just in time to see a huge wild boar, sneering and snarling at them. The boar looked a bit like a pig, only much bigger and hairier. On either side of its mouth were two long, razor-sharp white tusks. As Kristoff began to back away from the boar, Olaf ran straight at it.

"Oh, look! How cute!" Olaf said happily. He reached out a stick arm. "I think I'll pet this little guy. . . ."

"Olaf, no!" Kristoff grabbed Olaf just as the boar lunged forward. "Careful. I'm not sure this pig is very friendly."

Elsa stood slowly. She didn't want to make any sudden movements. But as she started to back away, she noticed more beady eyes staring at her. The boar wasn't alone. A whole herd of beasts had wandered out of the desert. They must have snuck up behind the group as they sat beside the dried-up lake.

"Use your powers, Elsa!" Anna hissed. She gave Elsa's shoulder a nudge.

Elsa reached out an arm, and a wall of ice shot up from the ground, forming a barrier between her friends and the boar. Elsa sighed in relief. Then she watched in dismay as the ice began to melt under the glare of the Eldora sun.

"Oh, no," Elsa said. "Not again!"

"What's wrong, Elsa?" Anna asked. "Why isn't it working?"

"The Summer Queen!" Elsa said. "Her magic is so strong. Nothing stays frozen in this heat!"

Elsa realized that her attempts to make ice had only confused and angered the boar. Now the entire growling, snarling herd was closing in.

Olaf took a few steps forward. "Guys, it's fine," he said. "You go ahead. I'll distract them."

Sven snorted and raised a hairy eyebrow in protest.

"I don't think so, Olaf," Kristoff said

softly. "When I say so, everyone is going to run back to the boat, okay? Ready? Go!"

Elsa and Anna raced to the boat as fast as their legs would carry them. Once everyone was inside, Kristoff snapped the reins. "Go, Sven!" he hollered. "GO!"

Sven let out a loud whinny and took off, dragging the boat across the dunes.

"Keep trying, Elsa!" Anna shouted.

Elsa leaned out of the boat, still attempting to use her powers. But each time she formed a wall of ice, it began to melt right away. The boars charged straight through it.

"I'm trying, Anna!" Elsa called out. She summoned her powers again and again, frantically trying to keep the pack of boars at bay. But she couldn't make the ice quickly enough to slow the boars down.

"Hold on, guys!" Kristoff shouted. "We're almost out of here!"

The little wooden boat crested over one last huge sand dune. Beyond the sand, Elsa could see small patches of grass and pointy shrubs. In the distance, she saw rolling brown hills and mountains. They were approaching the edge of Eldora's desert. She could just make out the rooftops of the royal city. "Finally!" she cried.

Suddenly, an arrow sailed in a wide arc over Elsa's head.

"Look at that!" Olaf said, his mouth hanging open in wonder.

Elsa turned to look over her shoulder. The arrow had landed in the sand, narrowly missing one of the beasts. One by one, the boars retreated into the desert, afraid to continue their advance.

Elsa breathed a sigh of relief as the boat slowed to a stop. They had reached the Eldora hills.

Chapter 8

"That was another close call," Anna said, stepping out of the boat. She walked over to Sven and gently patted his head. "Where did that arrow come from?"

"I have no idea," Elsa replied. She climbed out of the boat and looked around. In the distance she could see a magnificent castle nestled into the side of a mountain. It sparkled in the sunlight.

"Wow! Look at that!" Elsa said with a smile. She was finally going to meet the Summer Queen! Just as she took a few steps forward, she saw a young villager approaching. He was carrying a bow and a quiver of arrows.

"Sorry about the boars!" the villager called out cheerfully, waving the quiver above his head.

"It was you!" Elsa said gratefully. "You're the one who shot the arrow!"

"Nice work!" Kristoff agreed.

The villager smiled. "I'm Alvan. Welcome to the village of Eldora!"

"Thank you, Alvan," Elsa said. "I'm Queen Elsa of Arendelle, and these are my friends."

"Your Majesty," Alvan said, bending into a deep bow. "Forgive me, but I must return to my post. It's my job to make sure that no wild animals enter the town." With that, Alvan disappeared around a corner, leaving Elsa and her friends to explore.

Elsa took in the town. It was different from anything she'd ever seen. In Arendelle, all the houses had pointy roofs. But in Eldora, the roofs were flat. In Arendelle, the streets were made of bricks and cobblestones. In Eldora, the streets were dusty. In Arendelle, the castle was made of gray stones and green turrets. The buildings in Eldora were beautiful, but every one of them was brown.

"Look at that," Elsa said. "It looks like the entire village is made of . . . *sand*!"

"Not for long," Anna said with a wink. "Let's go help this Summer Queen."

Elsa and her friends set off for the castle, traveling along a dusty dirt road. Soon they happened upon another young villager. He was a shepherd, tending to his flock. A baby lamb wandered over to Olaf and gave him a playful lick on the cheek.

"Hey, that tickles!" Olaf said with a giggle.

Elsa and Anna laughed.

"Sorry about that," the shepherd said with a smile. "My sheep love meeting new people. It appears as though your sheep enjoys meeting new people, too."

"Please don't worry," Elsa said. "Only, this isn't a sheep. This is Olaf."

The shepherd furrowed his brow and gave Olaf a quizzical look.

"I'm Olaf, and I like warm hugs," Olaf said, waving his stick arms to say hello.

The shepherd raised his eyebrows in surprise and took a few timid steps in Olaf's direction. Elsa leaned in and lowered her voice. "He's a snowman," she explained.

As Olaf and the shepherd got acquainted, Elsa looked around at the flock of fluffy white sheep. She knew that sheep's wool was used to make warm clothes and blankets. She couldn't imagine needing any of those things in Eldora, though. It was just too hot! She could feel the sweat beading up on her forehead again.

"We should keep going," Elsa said to her friends.

Anna agreed. "Maybe when we get to the castle, we can have a cool drink."

Elsa and her friends continued. They walked until they came upon an old woman sitting in front of a large contraption. It was shaped like a giant wooden picture frame. Hundreds of tiny threads stretched across the frame from one end to the other.

"Excuse me," Elsa said to the woman. "May I ask what you're making?"

The old woman smiled. "Greetings. I'm Farah. I'm using this loom to weave a carpet," she said. The woman picked up a small metal hook and used it to weave pieces of yarn through the strings. At the bottom of the loom, Elsa could see the beginnings of a beautiful blue-and-gold rug. It reminded her of the carpets she had seen in the marketplace near the harbor.

"This is lovely, Farah," Elsa said, carefully running her fingertips along the threads. "I've always wanted to learn how to weave."

The woman scooted over and patted the ground next to her. "Have a seat," she said kindly. "I'll show you how."

"Really?" Elsa said eagerly.

Farah nodded, and Elsa sat beside her. The woman handed Elsa the metal hook. Then she guided Elsa's hand over and under the threads, helping her weave the yarn.

"That's very good work," Farah said, nodding in approval. "You're a natural."

"Thank you," Elsa said. "You're a very good teacher."

Elsa stood and gave the old woman a polite smile before continuing on her way.

"You know," Kristoff said, leaning in

close to Elsa, "for a town trapped in an eternal summer, the villagers of Eldora all seem to be in excellent spirits."

"I know," Elsa said. "It's strange."

"No one seems the least bit worried," Anna agreed.

"Why would anyone be worried?" Olaf asked innocently.

Anna smiled. "Maybe they've been trapped in an eternal summer for so long that they don't remember what the other seasons are like."

Elsa was wondering if that could be true when she turned the corner. She gasped.

In front of her was a massive wall with two huge wooden gates. They had finally

reached the entrance to the castle. In front of the gates stood two guards. They wore impressive-looking uniforms and carried long swords, sheathed at their hips. "I guess we're about to find out," Elsa said.

She approached the guards. Then she cleared her throat and summoned her most important-sounding voice.

"I'm Queen Elsa of Arendelle," she announced. "I've come to meet the Summer Queen."

One of the guards bent in a noble bow. "It's a pleasure to meet you, Queen Elsa. Unfortunately, the Queen of Eldora is not at home. We expect her back shortly, but she has been traveling in foreign lands."

Elsa looked at her friends. Was the

Summer Queen's magic powerful enough to cause an eternal summer from as far away as foreign lands? And if not, who was responsible for all this magic?

Chapter 9

Elsa heard the faint sound of a trumpet playing.

In the distance, she saw orange and gold flags waving in the hot summer breeze. Behind the flags, she saw a caravan of horses and camels. They were traveling out of the desert, into town.

"You're in luck, Queen Elsa," the guard said. "Here comes our queen now."

Elsa felt her stomach flip-flop with anticipation. After a long journey, she was finally going to meet the Summer Queen! Her mind was flooded with thoughts. Would the Summer Queen be nice? Would she be welcoming? Would Elsa be able to help her and save Eldora?

As Elsa watched the caravan approach, she heard another trumpet. This one was much closer. She tilted her face to the sky and saw a knight with a long horn standing on top of the castle walls. Suddenly, the town of Eldora came alive! Villagers streamed out of their homes and lined up on either side of the road. Everyone was cheering and clapping. Elsa was reminded

of the day she had left Arendelle, when all of her villagers had come out to wish her farewell.

"It doesn't look like anyone is afraid of the Summer Queen," Anna whispered to Elsa.

Elsa thought back to her coronation, when she had accidentally covered the Great Hall in ice. The villagers of Arendelle had been frightened. But the Eldora townspeople didn't seem frightened at all. "Everyone seems really . . . *excited*," she said. "How strange."

Elsa stood on her tiptoes to get a glimpse of the Summer Queen. She was curious to know what she looked like, but it was difficult to see. Villagers crowded around Elsa, elbow to elbow, eagerly awaiting the arrival of their queen.

"Do you want to climb onto Sven's back?" Kristoff asked. "You might have a better view that way."

Just as Elsa was about to take Kristoff up on his offer, the crowd parted. Elsa saw a beautiful woman about her age, riding a large black horse. The woman had long dark hair, styled in a lovely braid. Her eyes were the color of chocolate. She was dressed in a shimmery orange dress. It was the color of saffron, one of the spices Elsa had seen in the market.

The woman slid down from her horse and waved happily to the villagers. She walked toward the palace, stopping to greet one of the guards.

"Omar," the woman said with a small nod. "How is everyone in Eldora?"

"Queen Marisol," the guard said with a bow. "The villagers of Eldora are well. They are grateful for your safe return."

Queen Marisol, Elsa said to herself. *The Summer Queen has a beautiful name!*

Suddenly, the queen looked into the crowd and locked eyes with Elsa. "And who do we have here, Omar?" she asked.

"Queen Marisol, this is Queen Elsa of Arendelle," Omar said. "And these are her friends. They have traveled all the way from Arendelle to meet you."

Marisol's eyes grew wide, and a huge

smile spread across her face. "Of course!" she said, clapping her hands together. "I've been hearing all about the beautiful white-haired queen, her sister, and the strange little snowman since dropping anchor in the Eldora harbor! I must have been traveling right behind you this whole time!" Marisol reached down and patted Olaf on the head. She pulled her hand away in wonder. "Oh! He's so cold!"

Olaf giggled.

Elsa, meanwhile, was delighted. Queen Marisol seemed so . . . *nice.* And she didn't seem to be having trouble controlling her powers at all. Although the air was still unbearably hot.

"I'm so happy you've come," Marisol

103

continued. "I trust you've had a pleasant journey?"

Anna let out a chuckle. Elsa thought she knew why. Their journey had definitely been *exciting,* but it hadn't always been pleasant. Elsa gave her sister a gentle poke in the ribs.

"Yes, thank you. It has certainly been an adventure," Elsa said diplomatically. "Queen Marisol, this is my sister, Anna, Princess of Arendelle. You've already met Olaf. These are our friends Kristoff and Sven."

Marisol greeted each of Elsa's friends kindly. Then she turned to speak to the villagers of Eldora. "I'd like to formally welcome our new friends from Arendelle.

The castle will host a feast tonight in their honor!"

The villagers of Eldora erupted into whoops, hollers, and cheers. Marisol turned back to Omar. "Now please, open the gates!" she cried.

Slowly, the gates to the palace began to swing open. Behind them was a beautiful stone plaza with a bubbling fountain at its center.

Marisol took Elsa and Anna by the hand. "I've met most of the kings in the area, but it's so nice to meet another queen," she said. "And a princess, too! Please, won't you come to the castle? I'm sure you and your friends are tired after such a long trip."

Elsa was a little confused. On the one hand, she was delighted to meet the Summer Queen. Marisol was kind to her villagers. And she was planning a feast in her visitors' honor. It seemed like she would make a wonderful friend. On the other hand, Elsa had seen the evidence of an eternal summer with her own two eyes. She couldn't quite figure it out.

Elsa looked at Anna. Anna gave her an encouraging look. Elsa took a deep breath. Then she leaned toward Marisol and whispered, "When my sister and I heard that the gates to your kingdom were closed, we thought it was because you hadn't yet learned how to control your . . . *magic.*"

Marisol stopped in her tracks. "My what?" she asked, clearly confused.

"You know," Anna chimed in. "Your magic? The spells of fire and heat?"

Marisol furrowed her brow in thought. Then she burst into a fit of giggles. "What do you mean?" she said, laughing. "I don't have any magical powers."

Elsa was amazed. "If you don't have powers, what about the heat?"

"And the sandstorm?" Anna asked.

"And the dried-up lake?" Kristoff chimed in.

Sven snorted and stamped his feet.

"Queen Marisol," Elsa said in her most serious voice. "My friends and I have traveled all the way from Arendelle to help rid Eldora of its eternal summer."

Marisol smiled. "That's very kind of you," she said. "But Eldora isn't trapped in an eternal summer. It's just always warm here. We have tropical weather year-round."

Marisol went on to explain that everything Elsa and her friends had seen was natural. It *was* hot in Eldora, but the villagers were used to the weather. Sandstorms were common, but they weren't all that different from rain or snowstorms.

"In fact," Marisol continued, "the only dangerous things around here are the wild boars. That's why we have villagers standing guard with bows and arrows."

Elsa couldn't believe it. All this time, she had been convinced that the people of Eldora were in danger. Now she was discovering that there wasn't any danger after all.

A serious look spread across Marisol's face. "I hope you're not disappointed to find out that I'm only a regular queen," she said quietly.

Chapter 10

"Of course I'm not disappointed!" Elsa cried. She took Marisol's hands in hers and gave them a reassuring squeeze. How could she possibly be disappointed? She had a wonderful new friend. And she was delighted that the people of Eldora were happy.

"*I* don't have any powers," Anna told Marisol jokingly. "Elsa seems to like *me*."

Marisol chuckled. She seemed to be feeling better already. Elsa, however, was a little embarrassed. After all, she had come to Eldora because she'd thought the Summer Queen was in danger. After Olaf had gone on and on about Summer Land, what was she supposed to think?

Suddenly, Elsa turned to Olaf. She raised an eyebrow at him.

"Olaf . . . ," Elsa began.

"Yes?" Olaf said innocently.

"Olaf, I need you to tell me everything you heard about Summer Land."

"Okay!" Olaf said, waving his stick arms around in excitement. "One day, I was visiting with the ice harvesters. They were talking all about the kingdom of

Eldora, where it's always summer—"

"Pardon me for interrupting," Marisol said suddenly, "but did you say *ice harvesters*?"

Elsa and Olaf nodded. "Yes!" Olaf said.

"You have ice in your village?" she asked.

"Yes!" Olaf said again.

Marisol clapped her hands together and hopped up and down in delight. "It's the most wonderful news!" she said happily. She grabbed Elsa's and Anna's hands and danced around with them in a circle.

"What is it, Marisol?" Elsa asked.

"This is exactly why I have been visiting neighboring kingdoms!" Marisol

exclaimed. "We need ice to keep our fish fresh and to preserve our crops. I had been hoping to trade with another village, but there wasn't any ice to be found!"

Elsa's face broke into a huge grin. She thought she had come to Eldora to help end an eternal summer. Now she realized she could help in a different way. She was delighted.

"Marisol, we have all the ice you could ever want in Arendelle," Elsa said eagerly. "Why, Kristoff here is an expert. He knows more about ice than anyone I've ever met!"

Kristoff's cheeks turned bright red. Sven snorted in protest.

"Sven knows a lot about ice, too," Elsa said, petting Sven's head. She turned back to Marisol. "I would be happy to send you all the ice you need."

Marisol's eyes teared up in gratitude. She threw her arms around Elsa's neck. "Thank you!" she said. "You have made me and the people of Eldora happier than you know."

*

News of the partnership between Arendelle and Eldora spread quickly through the village. At the evening feast, villagers presented Elsa and her friends with gift after gift to show their thanks. Anna and Elsa received presents of sugar, spices, and beautiful jewelry. Kristoff and Sven were given woven rugs and carpets, which would come in handy in the chilly Arendelle winters.

Elsa smiled. The grand ballroom of the Eldora castle was filled with people singing, dancing, and eating. Everyone was having a splendid time.

Then Marisol leaned over the arm of her throne to speak to Elsa. "When you arrived in Eldora, you said you thought I needed help learning to control my magic," she said. "But I've never known anyone with powers before. So that got me thinking. . . ." Marisol paused and peered into Elsa's eyes. "Do *you*?"

Elsa took a deep breath. She wasn't sure

she should tell Marisol the truth. After all, they hadn't been friends for very long. What if Marisol was frightened?

Anna gave Elsa a tap on the shoulder. "It's okay," Anna said. "You can do it."

Elsa nodded. Anna was right. She slowly stood up from her chair and made her way to the center of the room.

Elsa was a little bit nervous. Even though she was a queen, she was still getting used to being the center of attention. Now everyone was staring at her. She took a deep breath. She smoothed the front of her dress with her hands. Then she gingerly pointed her foot and tapped her shoe once against the floor.

All of a sudden, the entire floor of the Eldora palace was covered in ice, just like a skating rink! Elsa could hear the collective gasp of the villagers. They had never seen anything like it before. There was a sudden chorus of claps and cheers and whistles. People began to slide across the ice in wonder. Some of them even dropped to their knees to feel the chill against their hands and cheeks.

Elsa raised her arms high, and a flurry of snowflakes rained down from the ceiling. Villagers stuck out their tongues, gleefully catching snowflakes in their mouths. Others formed snowballs or began making little snowmen in honor of

Olaf. Elsa gave a small, shy curtsey and returned to her chair amid a thunderous round of applause. Anna gave her an approving wink.

"That was incredible," Marisol said, shaking her head in disbelief. She grabbed Elsa's hand. "Elsa, you are a great queen. I am honored to call you my friend."

Elsa beamed with pride. The trip to Eldora hadn't gone as planned, but she was glad she had made the journey. She had traveled the seas. She had visited foreign lands. She had made a wonderful new friend in Marisol. And she had helped the villagers of Eldora. Maybe Olaf had been right after all. Summer Land had turned out to be a wonderful place!

Elsa was happy to see that her magic wasn't melting quite so fast now that she was inside the castle. But whenever it began to melt, she simply tapped her foot and a new layer of ice spread across the floor.

*

The following morning, Elsa and Anna exited the palace and prepared to say goodbye to the Summer Queen.

"I'll arrange for a shipment of ice just as soon as we arrive home," Elsa said to Marisol.

Marisol took Elsa's hand. "I will miss you so much. Please return to Eldora as soon as you can."

"We will," Elsa said. "But I insist that you come to Arendelle for a visit as well."

Marisol gave Elsa another big hug. Then she threw her arms around Anna. "You are so lucky to have each other," Marisol said. "Take care. Farewell."

Elsa and Anna lifted their arms and waved to the people of Eldora. Villagers had turned up by the hundreds to say goodbye. Elsa realized that she felt a little sad.

"I'm really going to miss Eldora and Queen Marisol," she said with a sigh.

"I am too," Anna said, taking her sister by the arm. "But do you want to hear a secret?"

"Sure," Elsa said.

Anna leaned in close to Elsa and whispered in her ear. "I can't *wait* for winter."

Elsa and Anna laughed and, arm in arm, began their long journey home.

Erica David has written more than forty books and comics for young readers, including Marvel Adventures *Spider-Man: The Sinister Six*. She graduated from Princeton University and is an MFA candidate at the Writer's Foundry in Brooklyn. She has always had an interest in all things magical, fantastic, and frozen, which has led her to work for Nickelodeon, Marvel, and an ice cream parlor, respectively. She resides sometimes in Philadelphia and sometimes in New York, with a canine familiar named Skylar.